# BAD KITTY

## DOES NOT LIKE
## VALENTINE'S DAY

### NICK BRUEL

ROARING BROOK PRESS
New York

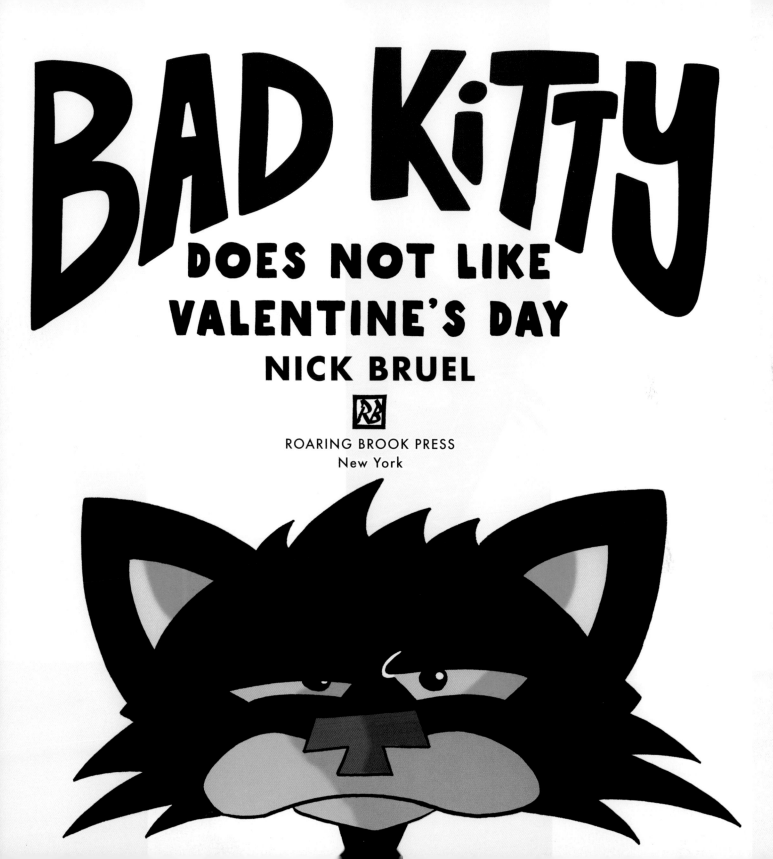

Kitty is not happy.

Today is Valentine's Day, but no one has given her a valentine.

Think about it, Kitty.
Think about all the things you've done
since **LAST** Valentine's Day.

Do you remember last **Easter**,
when you stole all the eggs?

Kitty remembers.

Do you remember last **Thanksgiving**, when you ate all the turkey?

*BURP!*

Kitty remembers.

Do you remember last **Christmas**, when you toppled the tree?

Kitty remembers.

Kitty remembers everything.
But now Kitty is worried.

Kitty is worried that . . .

. . . no one loves her.

If you want to **GET** a valentine, Kitty,
maybe you should **GIVE** a valentine.

Why don't you make a valentine for Puppy?
Puppy loves valentines!

Kitty is going to try.

Roses are red,
Violets are blue,
Sugar is sweet,

**YOU DROOL EVERYWHERE!
PLEASE STOP!
IT'S DISGUSTING!**

Roses are red,
Violets are blue,
Sugar is sweet,

**I GUESS
I THINK
I SUPPOSE
I LIKE YOU.**

Look at how happy you made Puppy!

Now he has a valentine
for **YOU**!

Roses are red,
Violets are blue,
Sugar is sweet,

Kitty **LOVES** her valentine!

But Kitty does not like
Valentine's Day.